BC 19462

DISCARDED

GREAT AFRICAN-AMERICAN WOMEN

Halle Berry

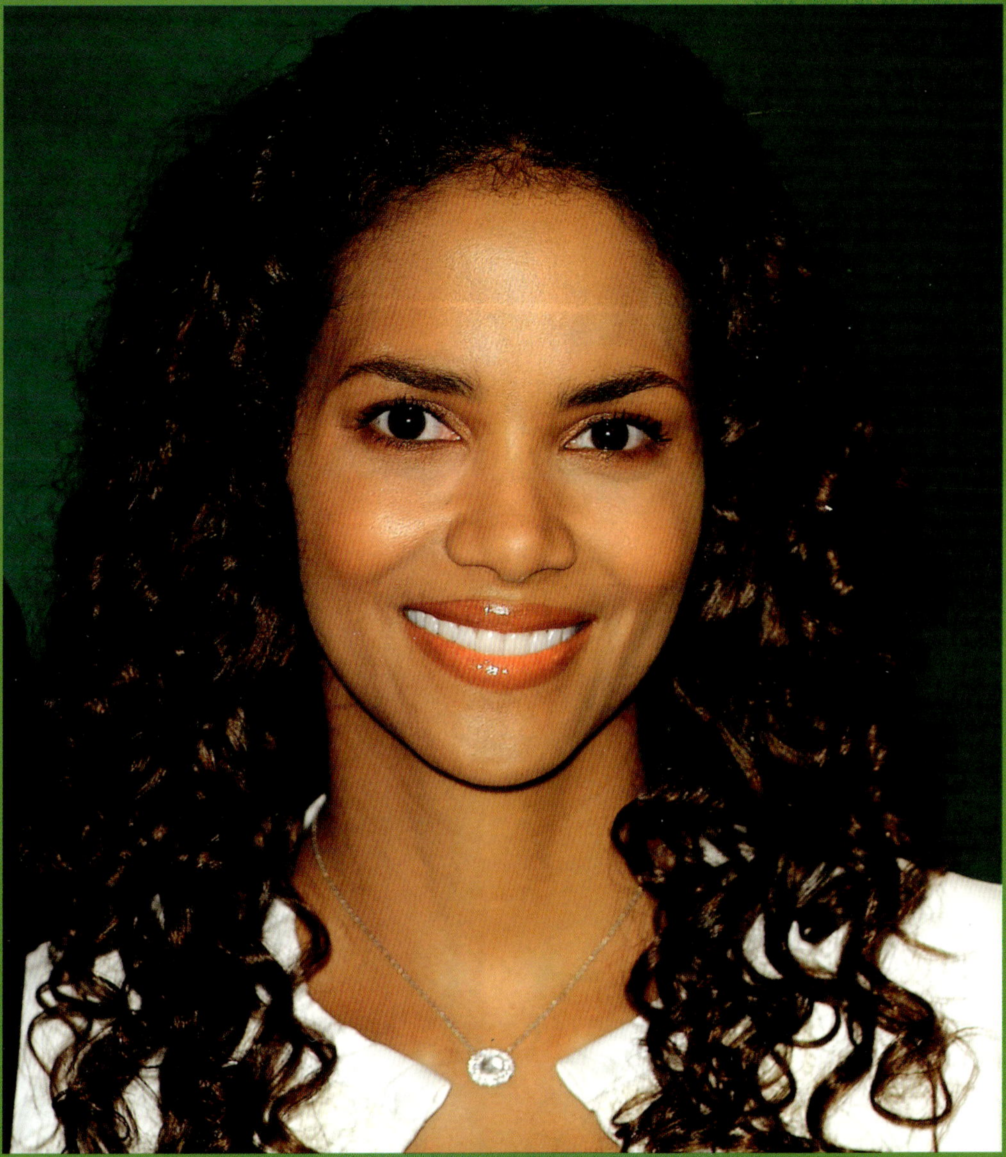

Erinn Banting

Published by Weigl Publishers Inc.
350 5th Avenue, Suite 3304, PMB 6G
New York, NY USA 10118-0069
Web site: www.weigl.com

Copyright 2006 WEIGL PUBLISHERS INC.
All rights reserved. No part of this publication may be reproduced, stored in a retrieval system, or transmitted in any form or by any means, electronic, mechanical, photocopying, recording, or otherwise, without the prior written permission of Weigl Publishers Inc.

All of the Internet URLs given in the book were valid at the time of publication. However, due to the dynamic nature of the Internet, some addresses may have changed, or sites may have ceased to exist since publication. While the author and publisher regret any inconvenience this may cause readers, no responsibility for any such changes can be accepted by either the author or the publisher.

Library of Congress Cataloging-in-Publication Data

Banting, Erinn.
  Halle Berry / Erinn Banting.
    p. cm. -- (Great African American women)
  Includes index.
  ISBN 1-59036-333-7 (hard cover : alk. paper) -- ISBN 1-59036-339-6 (soft cover : alk. paper)
 1. Berry, Halle--Juvenile literature. 2. Motion picture actors and actresses--United States--Juvenile literature. 3. African American motion picture actors and actresses--Juvenile literature. I. Title. II. Series.
 PN2287.B4377B36 2005
 791.4302'8'092--dc22

                                            2004029957

Printed and bound in the United States of America
1 2 3 4 5 6 7 8 9 0   09 08 07 06 05

Project Coordinator Janice L. Redlin
Copy Editor Tina Schwartzenberger
Design Terry Paulhus **Layout** Kathryn Livingstone
Photo Research Kim Winiski and Annalise Bekkering

Photograph Credits
Every reasonable effort has been made to trace ownership and to obtain permission to reprint copyright material. The publishers would be pleased to have any errors or omissions brought to their attention so that they may be corrected in subsequent printings.

Cover: Halle Berry is one of the most well-known African-American actresses in the world today.

Cover: Getty Images/Carlos Alvarez (front); Getty Images/Lucy Nicholson/AFP (back);
Corbis: page 8 (Lynne Sladky/Bettman);
Getty Images: pages 1 (Steve Finn), 3 (Carlos Alvarez), 4 (Kurt Vinion), 5 (Lucy Nicholson/AFP), 6T (Steve Finn), 6B (Panoramic Images), 7T (Comstock Images), 7M (David Rosenberg/Stone), 7B (Paul Spinelli), 12 (Sean Gallup), 13TL (Burke/Triolo Productions/Brand X Pictures), 13TR (Thinkstock), 13B (Photodisc Blue), 14 (Eric Ford/Online USA), 15 (Ernst Haas/Hulton Archive), 16 (Jon Kopaloff), 17 (Frank Micelotta), 18 (David McNew/Newsmakers), 19T (Vince Bucci/AFP), 19B (Frederick M. Brown), 21T (Gene Lester/Hulton Archive), 21M (Duncan Smith/Taxi), 21BL (Timothy A. Clary/AFP), 21BR (Getty Sports), 22T (C Squared Studios/Photodisc Green), 22M (Siede Preis/Photodisc Green); **Heather C. Hudak:** page 22B; **Photofest:** pages 9, 11, 20; **Photos.com:** page 10.

GREAT AFRICAN-AMERICAN WOMEN

Halle Berry

CONTENTS

Who is Halle Berry?........................ 5
Growing Up in Cleveland 6
Learning to Act 8
Becoming an Actor 10
What is Movie Making? 12
Movies in Hollywood...................... 14
Overcoming Obstacles 16
Special Achievements 18
Halle in Movies 20
Time Line 21
Making a Flip Book 22
Further Research........................... 23
Words to Know/Index..................... 24

Who is Halle Berry?

Halle Berry is a well-known actress. She was born in Cleveland, Ohio. When she finished **college**, Halle moved to Chicago, Illinois, to become an actress. Since then, she has starred in television shows and movies. People around the world have seen Halle act.

Halle has faced many struggles because of her culture. It was difficult to obtain movie roles that are not traditionally given to African-American women. Halle is the first African-American woman to win an **Academy Award** for best actress. Her struggles and **successes** have **inspired** many young African Americans to become actors.

> I don't see a white woman. I see a black woman, even though my mother is white. Knowing that has made my life easier, I think.

Growing Up in Cleveland

Halle's mother named her after a department store in Cleveland called Halle Brothers Department Store. Her early years growing up in Cleveland were difficult. Halle's parents were separated. She did not see her father. Halle lived with her mother and sister. Halle's mother was a nurse. She took care of her daughters by herself.

When Halle's parents divorced, her mother moved the family to an area outside the center of Cleveland. Moving to a new home and school was difficult for Halle at first. Her family and teachers helped her. Halle began exploring her love of art, music, and acting.

Halle visits Cleveland regularly to see her mother and sister.

OHIO Tidbits

   Cardinal   Buckeye 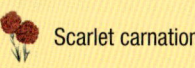 Scarlet carnation

FLAG SEAL BIRD TREE FLOWER

OHIO — Cleveland, Columbus

The first traffic light in the United States was located in Cleveland.

Ohio is the United States's leading producer of greenhouse and nursery plants.

In 1879, Cleveland became the first city lighted by electricity.

The first hot dog came from Ohio. It was invented by Harry M. Stevens.

Seven American presidents were born in Ohio. They are Ulysses S. Grant, Rutherford B. Hayes, James A. Garfield, Benjamin Harrison, William McKinley, William H. Taft, and Warren G. Harding.

Oberlin College was founded in 1833 in Ohio. It was the first college in the United States to educate all cultures and both males and females.

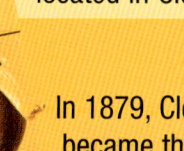

The Rock and Roll Hall of Fame is located in Cleveland.

Think about it!

How might living in the state of Ohio have influenced Halle? Research your state's sites and symbols, and write about how they might have influenced you and your family.

Halle Berry

Learning to Act

One of Halle's friends recognized Halle's beauty and talent. The friend entered Halle in the Miss Teen Ohio **pageant** in 1984. Halle won the contest. She won many other pageants after that. Still, Halle wanted to be a **journalist**. She studied at the Cuyahoga Community College in Cleveland.

Halle enjoyed college, but decided not to look for work as a journalist. Instead, she moved to Chicago to work as a model. Halle realized that acting was what she really wanted to do. In Chicago, Halle **auditioned** for a part in a television show called *Angels '88*. She did not receive the part.

Halle represented Ohio in the 1986 Miss USA Pageant. She was awarded the first runner-up position.

Halle Berry
Quick Facts

Halle won an Academy Award for her role in *Monster's Ball*. She dedicated the Oscar to all the African-American actresses that came before her.

In the movie *Die Another Day*, Halle said, "I play the feminine James Bond. She's the next step in the evolution of women in the Bond movies. She's more modern—more intelligent—and not the classic villain."

Halle is pleased her career is growing. "One of the greatest results is the fact I'm getting some really great parts."

In 1989, Halle acted in a television show called *Living Dolls*. Since then, her acting abilities have become recognized. Halle has acted in a variety of movies ranging from drama to action. She had roles in the dramas *Jungle Fever* (1991) and *Monster's Ball* (2002). Halle also acted in the action movies *X-Men* (2000) and *Catwoman* (2004).

Halle provided the voice for Cappy, one of the animated characters in the 2005 movie *Robots*.

Becoming an Actor

Actors take classes to learn how to play different roles. Classes help them learn how to look and sound like their characters.

For her part in the film *Introducing Dorothy Dandridge*, Halle took acting classes. The movie is about an African-American actress who worked in the 1950s and 1960s. Halle studied Dorothy Dandridge's diaries, letters, and photographs to understand her character.

In movies such as *X-Men*, Halle wore makeup to help her fit the part. For other characters she has played, Halle has worn costumes. When she played Catwoman, Halle wore a leather suit that made her look like a cat. She also learned how to move like a cat.

Acting Tips

Actors must communicate with the audience.

Qualifications
- ☑ good memory
- ☑ alert
- ☑ clear and strong voice
- ☑ speak clearly; controlled breathing

Training
- ☑ must be able to relax
- ☑ must be able to concentrate
- ☑ must control body and voice

Tasks
- ☑ determine desires of character
- ☑ determine actions to achieve the desires
- ☑ able to convincingly perform the actions

Tips
- ☑ do not become nervous
- ☑ practice makes perfect; work regularly at practicing the lines of the character

To prepare for her role in *Catwoman*, Halle studied fighting for more than 3 months. She learned a Brazilian martial art called Capoeira, which combines dance and gymnastic movements with martial arts.

What is Movie Making?

Writers, directors, **producers**, crewmembers, actors, and editors work hard to make movies. Movies can take months or even years to create. They have been made in the United States since the early 1900s. The first movies were called silent films because they did not have sound.

There are many jobs that need to be filled on a movie set. Some positions include actors, directors, camera crews, and even animal trainers.

Many people help make movies. Every person involved has different tasks. Halle works with each of these people when she acts in movies.

Screenplay

The first step in making a movie is writing a **script**, or screenplay. Writers often work together to create the characters and action in movies.

Director

After a script is written, the director reads it. Directors decide what they want the movie to look and sound like.

Producer

The producer also reads the script. Producers organize the director, cast, and crew. Producers also choose locations and make schedules for filming the movie. They make sure the movie costs are on **budget**. Once the film is made, producers organize the editing and **release**.

Editor

Editors put all the scenes in order. Sometimes, the first scenes filmed take place at the end of the movie. Often, some scenes are left out of the movie.

Halle Berry 13

Movies in Hollywood

Hollywood is a district in California. It is a part of the city of Los Angeles and is the world capital of the moviemaking industry. Many actors, directors, and producers live there. They make the city an exciting and glamorous place. Many of the movies Halle acts in are made in Hollywood.

A bus was lifted in the air by cranes to make a fake crash scene for the movie *Swordfish*. Halle acted in this movie in 2001.

Hollywood
Quick Facts

Nickname: Tinseltown

Claim to Fame: The Hollywood Walk of Fame

The Walk of Fame is located on Hollywood Boulevard. Tile stars have been built into a 10-block stretch of sidewalk. There are more than 2,000 stars. Each star has the name of an actor, artist, or musician on it. The Walk of Fame is one of the most-visited tourist sites in Hollywood.

Movie cameras quickly take a series of pictures called frames. These frames are normally shown at 24 frames per second. This speed makes the subjects look like they are moving.

By the 1920s, movies had grown popular with audiences. At this time, major film studios, many of which still make movies today, began to open in Hollywood. People from around the world came to Hollywood to work. People still come to Hollywood to make films.

Overcoming Obstacles

Halle is one of the most popular and successful actresses in Hollywood. Growing up, Halle did not always fit in. Halle's mother was of European ancestry, and her father was African American. When Halle grew up in the 1960s and 1970s, African-American people faced **racism** in many parts of the United States. Some people believed that people of different cultures should not marry and have children. Many people treated Halle poorly because of her mixed background.

Halle's achievements have made her a role model for many people.

In 1989, Halle was diagnosed with **diabetes**. People need **insulin** to help their bodies turn the food they eat into energy. Many people with diabetes live healthy lives. Halle helps educate people about diabetes through volunteer work with the American Diabetes Association. This group helps people who have the disease.

Halle credits her success to living with diabetes. She feels the disease has given her the strength she has needed to overcome obstacles in her life.

Halle often makes public appearances to draw attention to diabetes. In 2004, she participated in a benefit with Barbara Davis for the Barbara Davis Center for Childhood Diabetes.

Special Achievements

Halle has had a big impact in Hollywood. She has changed people's perceptions of African Americans. In Halle's early career, she competed in pageants, such as Miss Teen Ohio, Miss USA, and Miss World. Halle showed people that women from all cultures and backgrounds are beautiful. She won movie roles that were not traditionally given to African-American women, including Catwoman.

By 2005, Halle had won nearly twenty acting awards.

After winning the Golden Globe Award for her role as Dorothy Dandridge, Halle began receiving leading roles in major motion pictures.

Halle has received several awards. Her awards include a **Golden Globe Award** and an **Emmy Award** for her role in *Introducing Dorothy Dandridge*. Halle also won an Academy Award for her role in *Monster's Ball*.

Halle has won the Essence Award for excellence in film. This award honors powerful African Americans.

Halle Berry

Halle in Movies

Halle has starred in more than twenty movies. Here is a list of all the movies in which Halle has acted:

Jungle Fever (1991)
The Last Boy Scout (1991)
Strictly Business (1991)
Boomerang (1992)
Father Hood (1993)
The Program (1993)
The Flintstones (1994)
Losing Isaiah (1995)
Executive Decision (1996)
Girl 6 (1996)
Race the Sun (1996)
The Rich Man's Wife (1996)
B.A.P.S. (1997)
Bulworth (1998)
Why Do Fools Fall in Love? (1998)
X-Men (2000)
Swordfish (2001)
Die Another Day (2002)
Monster's Ball (2002)
Gothika (2003)
X2: X-Men United (2003)
Catwoman (2004)
Robots (2005)

The popularity of the movie *X-Men* led to a sequel. *X2: X-Men United* was released in 2003.

Time Line

DECADE	HALLE BERRY	WORLD EVENTS
1960s	Halle is born August 14, 1966, in Cleveland, Ohio.	In 1966, Walt Disney, creator of Disneyland, dies.
1980s	In 1984, Halle wins the Miss Teen Ohio pageant. Halle acts in a 1989 television show called *Living Dolls*. Halle collapses on stage in 1989 after developing diabetes.	In 1984, the Acquired Immune Deficiency Syndrome (AIDS) disease is identified.
2000s	In 2000, Halle wins the Emmy Award for outstanding lead actress for her role in *Introducing Dorothy Dandridge*. Halle wins an Oscar award for best actress at the Academy Awards in 2002 for her role in *Monster's Ball*. In 2004, Halle acts in the movie *Catwoman*.	In 2000, George W. Bush wins the presidential election in the United States. Queen Elizabeth II of the United Kingdom celebrates 50 years as queen of the **Commonwealth** in 2002. Athens, Greece, hosts the summer Olympics in 2004.

Halle Berry

Making a Flip Book

Films are made up of thousands of frames, or pictures. Each picture is slightly different. The pictures are run very quickly through a machine called a projector. This makes it look like the people on the frames are moving. A flip book is a way to make your own movie.

Materials

twenty small pieces of paper or cue cards

markers

stapler

1. Draw a circle on each of the cue cards. Try to draw the circles in the same place on each card. The circle will be the face of the character in the movie.

2. On the first card, draw eyes, a nose, and a mouth.

3. On each of the other cards, change the eyes and mouth a small amount. You can make your character smile or wink.

4. Staple the cards together on the left side. Flip through your book.

Now you have created a fun way to see how movies work.

Further Research

Further Reading

O'Brien, Daniel. *Halle Berry*. Surrey, United Kingdom: Reynolds & Hearn Limited, 2003.

Parish, James Robert. *Halle Berry: Actor*. New York, NY: Ferguson Publishing Company, 2004.

Web Sites

To learn more about Halle's life and career, log on to these sites.

Halle Berry's Fan Club
www.hallewood.com

Internet Movie Database Inc.
www.imdb.com/name/nm0000932

Words to Know

Academy Award: an acting award for movie performers

auditioned: a performer or group displayed their skills in a movie, play, or television show in a trial performance

budget: amount of money available for a project

college: a school of higher learning that people attend after high school

Commonwealth: a group of nations that share a common interest

diabetes: a disease that stops the body from producing insulin

Emmy Award: an award for television performers

Golden Globe Award: an award for movie and television performers

inspired: having an idea, feeling, or reason to do something

insulin: a hormone that controls the amount of sugar in a person's body

journalist: a person who reports the news

pageant: a contest that showcases people's talents

producers: people who supervise movies, plays, or television shows

racism: dislike of a person because of his or her culture

release: make available to the public

script: the written version of a play or a movie

successes: a favorable performance or achievement

Index

Academy Award.....5, 9, 19, 21

Catwoman............9, 11, 20, 21
Chicago, Illinois................5, 8
Cleveland, Ohio....5, 6, 7, 8, 21
Cuyahoga Community
   College................................8

Dandridge,
   Dorothy..................10, 19, 21
diabetes..........................17, 21

Emmy Award..................19, 21

Golden Globe Award............19

Halle Brothers Department
   Store 6
Hollywood..........14, 15, 16, 18

Miss Teen Ohio..........8, 18, 21
Miss USA.......................8, 18
Miss World...........................18
movies 5, 9, 10, 12, 13,
   14, 15, 18, 20, 21